Parents and Caregivers,

Here are a few ways to support your beginning rea

- Talk with your child about the ideas addressed in the story.
- Discuss each illustration, mentioning the characters, where they are, and what they are doing.
- Read with expression, pointing to each word.
- Talk about why the character did what he or she did and what your child would do in that situation.
- Help your child connect with characters and events in the story.

Remember, reading with your child should be fun, not forced.

Gail Saunders-Smith, Ph.D

Padres y personas que cuidan niños,

Aquí encontrarán algunas formas de apoyar al lector que recién se inicia:

- Hable con su niño/a sobre las ideas desarrolladas en el cuento.
- Discuta cada ilustración, mencionando los personajes, dónde se encuentran y qué están haciendo.
- Lea con expresión, señalando cada palabra.
- Hable sobre por qué el personaje hizo lo que hizo y qué haría su niño/a en esa situación.
- Ayude al niño/a a conectarse con los personajes y los eventos del cuento.

Recuerde, leer con su hijo/a debe ser algo divertido, no forzado.

Gail Saunders-Smith, Ph.D

BILINGUAL STONE ARCH **READERS**

are published by Stone Arch Books, a Capstone imprint
1710 Roe Crest Drive, North Mankato, Minnesota 56003
www.capstonepub.com

Library of Congress Cataloging-in-Publication data is available on the Library of Congress website.

ISBN: 978-1-4342-3775-0 (library binding)
ISBN: 978-1-4342-3914-3 (paperback)

Original Translation: Claudia Heck
Translation Services: Strictly Spanish

Reading Consultants:
Gail Saunders-Smith, Ph.D
Melinda Melton Crow, M.Ed
Laurie K. Holland, Media Specialist

Printed in the United States of America in North Mankato, Minnesota.
042018   000405

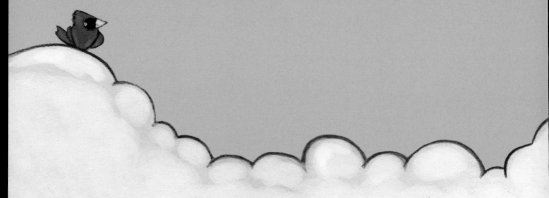

LÍOS EN LA NIEVE
SNOW TROUBLE

por/by
Melinda Melton Crow

ilustrado por/illustrated by
Ronnie Rooney

STONE ARCH BOOKS
a capstone imprint

This is Green Truck.
This is Dump Truck.
This is Blue Truck.

Este es Camión Verde.
Este es Camión Volcador.
Este es Camión Azul.

Green Truck sees trees.

Camión Verde ve árboles.

Dump Truck sees sand.

Camión Volcador ve arena.

Blue Truck sees snow.

Camión Azul ve nieve.

Oh, no! Do you see the ice?

¡Oh, no! ¿Ves el hielo?

"Oh, no!" says Blue Truck.
"I am sliding on the ice."

"¡Oh, no!" dice Camión Azul.
"Me estoy resbalando en el hielo".

"Help, help, help!" says Blue Truck.
"Who will stop me?"

"¡Ayuda, ayuda, ayuda!" dice
Camión Azul.
"¿Quién me parará?"

Green Truck and Dump Truck see
Blue Truck sliding.

Camión Verde y Camión Volcador ven
a Camión Azul resbalarse.

"I will stop you," says Dump Truck.

"Yo te pararé", dice Camión Volcador.

Dump Truck gets sand.

Camión Volcador carga arena.

"I will stop you too," says Green Truck.

"Yo también te pararé", dice Camión Verde.

Green Truck makes a snow pile.
Dump Truck drops the sand.

Camión Verde hace una pila de nieve.
Camión Volcador tira la arena.

Blue Truck stops sliding.

Camión Azul para de resbalarse.

"Thank you!" says Blue Truck.
"You are good pals."

"¡Gracias!" dice Camión Azul.
"Ustedes son buenos amigos".

story words

truck	sand	ice
dump	snow	help
trees	sliding	stop

palabras del cuento

camión	arena	hielo
volcador	nieve	ayuda
árboles	resbalarse	parar